Go, Dog. Go!

by P.D. Eastman

RANDOM HOUSE NEW YORK

To Cluny

Copyright © 1961 by P. D. Eastman.
Copyright renewed 1989 by Mary L. Eastman.
All rights reserved under International and Pan-American Copyright Conventions.
Published in the United States by Random House Children's Books,
a division of Random House, Inc., New York.

www.randomhouse.com/kids
www.kohlscorporation.com

This special edition was printed for Kohl's by Random House Children's Books,
a division of Random House, Inc., New York.

ISBN: 0-375-87521-2

Printed in the United States of America   10 9 8 7 6 5 4 3 2 1

RANDOM HOUSE and colophon are registered trademarks of Random House, Inc.

Dog.

Big dog.

Little dog.

Big dogs and little dogs.

Black and white dogs.

"Hello!"

"Hello!"

"Do you like my hat?"

"I
do
not."

"Good-by!"

"Good-by!"

One little dog going in.

Three big dogs going out.

A red dog
on a blue tree.

A blue dog
on a red tree.

A green dog

on a yellow tree.

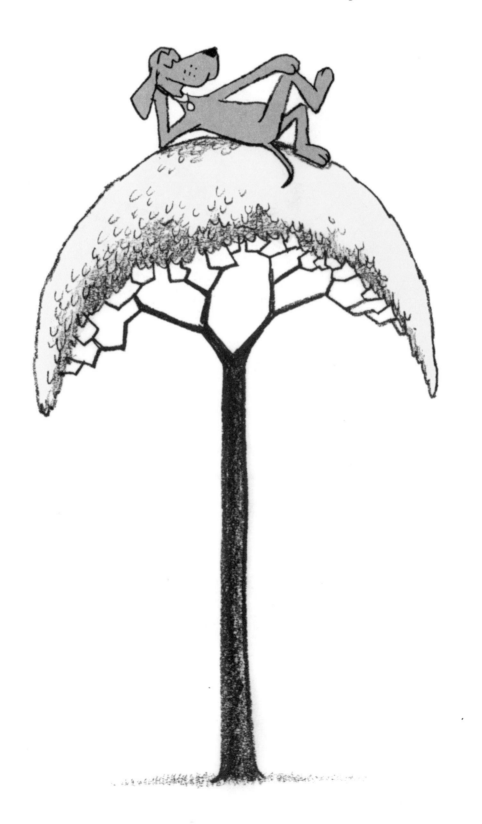

Some big dogs
and some little dogs
going around
in cars.

A dog

out of a car.

Two big dogs
going up.

One little dog
going down.

The   green   dog
is up.

The   yellow   dog
is down.

The blue dog
is in.

The red dog
is out.

One dog up
on a house.

Three dogs down
in the water.

A green dog
over a tree.

A yellow dog
under a tree.

Two dogs
in a house
on a boat
in the water.

A dog over the water.

A dog under the water.

"Hello again." "Hello."

"Do you like my hat?"

"I do not like it."

"Good-by again."

"Good-by."

The dogs
are all going
around,
and around,
and around.

"Go around
again!"

The sun is up.

The sun is yellow.

The yellow sun

is over the house.

"It is hot
out here in
the sun."

"It is not hot
here under the house."

Now it is night.

Three dogs
at a party
on a boat
at night.

Dogs at work.

Work, dogs,
work!

Dogs at play.

"Play, dogs, play!"

"Hello again."

"Hello."

"Do you
like my hat?"

"I do not
like that hat."

Dogs in cars again.

Going away.

Going away fast.

Look at those dogs go.

Go, dogs. Go!

"Stop, dogs. Stop!
The light is red now."

"Go, dogs. Go!
The light is green now."

Two dogs at play.

At play up on top.

"Go down, dogs.
Do not play up there.
Go down."

Now it is night.
Night is not
a time for play.

It is time for sleep.

The dogs go to sleep.

They will sleep all night.

Now it is day.

The sun is up.

Now is the time

for all dogs to get up.

"Get up!"

It is day.

Time to get going.

Go, dogs. Go!

There they go.

Look at those dogs go!

Why are they going fast
in those cars?
What are they going to do?
Where are those dogs going?

Look where they are going.
They are all going to that
big tree over there.

Now the cars stop.
Now all the dogs get out.
And now look where
those dogs are going!

To the tree! To the tree!

Up   the   tree!   Up   the   tree!

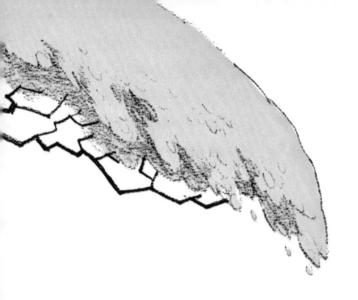

Up they go
to the top of the tree.
Why?
Will they work there?
Will they play there?
What is up there
on top of that tree?

A dog party!
A big dog party!
Big dogs, little dogs,
red dogs, blue dogs,
yellow dogs, green dogs,
black dogs, and white dogs
are all at a dog party!
What a dog party!

"Hello again.
And now
do you
like
my hat?"

"I do.
What a hat!
I like it!
I like
that party hat!"

"Good-by!"

"Good-by."